# Old Pig

*For my Mother*
*M.W.*

*Special Thanks to Rosalind Price,*
*to Margaret, Sam, Adelaide and Henry,*
*and to Paul Clark for Captain Taylor's paddock*
*R.B.*

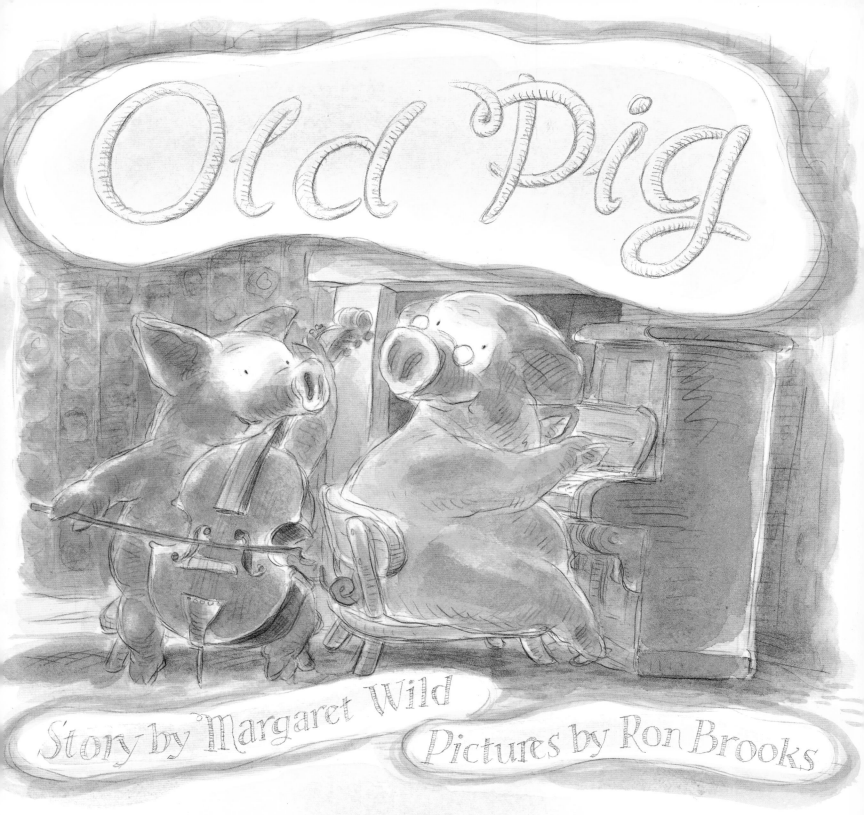

# Old Pig

Story by Margaret Wild    Pictures by Ron Brooks

Viking

Old Pig and Granddaughter had lived together for a long, long time.

They shared everything, including the chores.

Every day, Granddaughter chopped the wood, while Old Pig cleaned out the fire grate.

Granddaughter swept, while Old Pig dusted.

Old Pig made the beds, while Granddaughter hung up the washing.

Granddaughter made porridge,
tea and toast for breakfast.

Old Pig diced carrots and turnips for lunch.

And together Old Pig and Granddaughter prepared their dinner of corn and oats.

'I hate corn and oats,' Granddaughter always said.
And Old Pig always replied, 'Corn and oats are good for you.
While I'm alive, my dear, you'll eat them up.'

At that, Granddaughter stopped complaining.
She'd eat corn and oats for breakfast, lunch and dinner
if it meant that Old Pig would live forever.

One morning, Old Pig did not get up as usual for breakfast.

'I'm feeling tired,' she said. 'I think I'll have breakfast in bed today.'
'But you never eat in bed!' said Granddaughter.
'You don't like getting crumbs in the sheets.'
'I'm tired,' Old Pig repeated.

And when Granddaughter brought her a tray of porridge, toast and tea,
Old Pig was asleep, and she slept through lunch and dinner too.

While Old Pig slept, Granddaughter chopped the wood, cleaned out the fire grate, swept, dusted, did the washing and made her bed. She tried to whistle while she worked, but all she could manage was a lonely little 'oink'.

The next morning Old Pig was still tired, but she made herself get up.
She had a spoonful of porridge, a bite of toast and a sip of tea.

'That's not enough to feed a sparrow, let alone a big old pig like you,'
said Granddaughter. She pulled a funny, stern face, but Old Pig just shut
her eyes for a moment, then looked around for her bag and hat.

'I have a lot to do today,' she said. 'I must be prepared.'
'Prepared for what?' asked Granddaughter.

Old Pig didn't reply. She didn't have to. Granddaughter already
knew the answer and it made her feel like crying inside.

Old Pig returned her books to the library – and didn't borrow any more.
She went to the bank, took out all her money, and closed the account.

Then she went to the grocery store and paid the bill. She also paid
the electricity bill, the greengrocer's bill and the bill for firewood.

When she got home she tucked the rest of her money into Granddaughter's purse.
'Keep it safe,' she said, 'and use it wisely.'
'I will,' said Granddaughter. She tried to smile but her mouth wobbled,
and Old Pig said, 'There, there, no tears.'
'I promise,' said Granddaughter, but it was the hardest promise
she'd ever had to make.

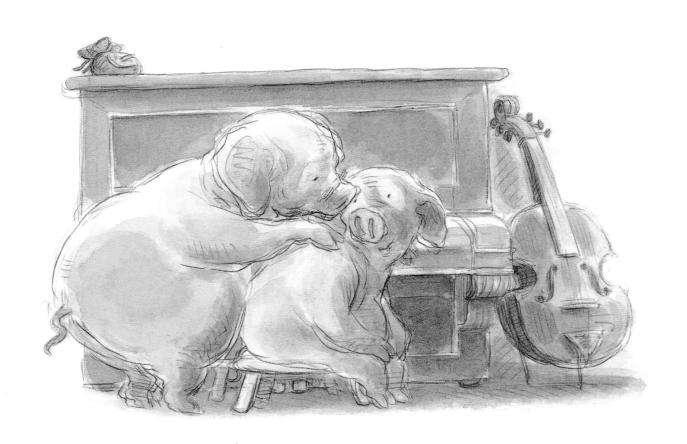

'Now,' said Old Pig, 'I want to feast.'
'You've got your appetite back?' Granddaughter asked, suddenly feeling hopeful.
'I'm not hungry for food,' Old Pig said, 'I want to take a slow walk around
the town and feast my eyes on the trees, the flowers, the sky – on everything!'

So Old Pig and Granddaughter went for a slow walk around the town.
Every now and again Old Pig had to stop and rest. But she kept on looking.
Looking and listening, smelling and tasting.

'Look!' said Old Pig.
'Do you see how the light glitters on the leaves?'

'Look!' said Old Pig.
'Do you see how the clouds gather like gossips in the sky?'

'Look!' said Old Pig.
'Do you see how the summer house is reflected in the lake?'

'Do you hear the parrots quarrelling?

Can you smell the warm earth?

Let's taste the rain!'

It was late by the time Old Pig and Granddaughter got home.

Old Pig was so exhausted that Granddaughter helped her straight into bed.

Then Granddaughter made herself a bowl of corn and oats,
and she ate them all up. She washed the dishes and put them away.

Then she went into Old Pig's room. Old Pig was not yet asleep.

Granddaughter sat beside her on the bed.
She said, 'Do you remember when I was little and had a bad dream,
you used to come into my bed and hold me tight?'
'I remember,' said Old Pig.

'Tonight,' said Granddaughter, 'I'd like to come into your bed
and hold you tight. Would that be all right?'
'That would be very all right,' said Old Pig.

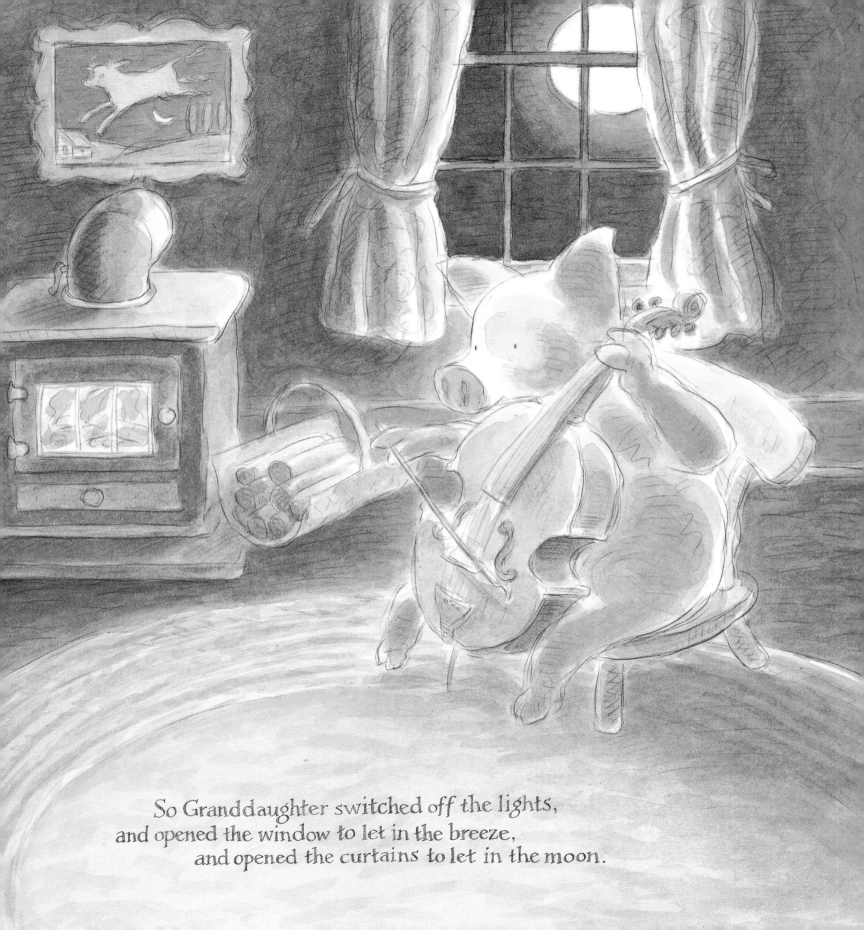

So Granddaughter switched off the lights,
and opened the window to let in the breeze,
and opened the curtains to let in the moon.

Then she climbed into Old Pig's bed.
She put her arms around Old Pig, and for the very last time
Old Pig and Granddaughter held each other tight until morning.

VIKING

Published by the Penguin Group
Penguin Books Ltd, 27 Wrights Lane, London W8 5TZ, England
Penguin Books USA Inc., 375 Hudson Street, New York, New York 10014, USA
Penguin Books Australia Ltd, Ringwood, Victoria, Australia
Penguin Books Canada Ltd, 10 Alcorn Avenue, Toronto, Ontario, Canada M4V 3B2
Penguin Books (NZ) Ltd, 182-190 Wairau Road, Auckland 10, New Zealand

Penguin Books Ltd, Registered Offices: Harmondsworth, Middlesex, England

First published in Australia by Allen & Unwin Pty Ltd 1995
First published in Great Britain by Viking 1996
1 3 5 7 9 10 8 6 4 2

Text copyright © Margaret Wild, 1995
Illustrations copyright © Ron Brooks, 1995

Designed by Ron Brooks

Made and printed by Toppan Printing Company, Singapore

A CIP catalogue record for this book is available from the British Library

ISBN 0-670-86706-3